MARY ENGELBREIT'S FAIRY TALES

TWELVE TIMELESS TREASURES

With an introduction by
LEONARD S. MARCUS

HARPER

An Imprint of HarperCollins Publishers

Heartfelt thanks to Pam, Jackie, Casey, Angela, Alexa, and
as always, Stephanie—what would I do without you?
—M.E.

Mary Engelbreit's Fairy Tales

Library of Congress Cataloging-in-Publication Data
Engelbreit, Mary.
     Mary Engelbreit's fairy tales : twelve timeless treasures / with an introduction by Leonard S. Marcus. — 1st ed.
          v.   cm.
     Contents: Cinderella — Beauty and the beast — Aladdin — Snow White and the seven dwarfs — The frog
prince — The little mermaid – The princess and the pea — Rapunzel — Thumbelina — Snow White and Rose Red
— Rumpelstiltskin — Sleeping Beauty.
     ISBN 978-0-06-088583-0 (trade bdg.)
     1. Fairy tales. [1. Fairy tales. 2. Folklore.] I. Title. II. Title: Fairy tales.
PZ8.E569Mar   2010   2009031214
398.2—dc22
[E]   CIP
                                                                                                             AC

Typography by Sarah Hoy
10 11 12 13 14   SCP   10 9 8 7 6 5 4 3 2 1
❖
First Edition

FOR MY
PRINCE
Charming,
PHILIP

TABLE of

CONTENTS

INTRODUCTION

Fairy tales are stories to grow on. They are stories that we never really outgrow. One of childhood's great adventures begins when first we fall, wide-eyed and rapt, under the spell of these simple-sounding yet richly evocative mini-narratives, with their unforgettable characters like Thumbelina and Aladdin and direct line to our most basic wishes and dreams. One of parenthood's signal pleasures comes, in turn, with the chance to rediscover these classic stories in the company of our own children. *Mary Engelbreit's Fairy Tales* is a well-lighted open door to that rewarding experience.

What do children of today see in old-fashioned, once-upon-a-time tales like "Rapunzel" and "The Princess and the Pea"? The youngest ones can be counted on—like generations of preschoolers before them—to delight in the tried-and-true, fun-to-imagine special effects:

Cinderella's magically transforming pumpkin-coach, Aladdin's wonderful lamp, the epic hundred-year nap taken by Sleeping Beauty and an entire castle population. Slightly older children—grade-schoolers proud to know something about how the real world works—are apt to be intrigued as well by the special rules that govern life in Fairy-tale Land: the fact that animals there can talk, for instance, and, as in "The Frog Prince," that no one seems the least bit surprised when they do. Ogres, witches, and fairy godmothers move about freely in this alternate universe. They, too, are taken completely for granted. Time and again, the stories stretch our idea of the possible in startling, often wished-for ways, opening our eyes and minds and hearts to one of life's big questions: "What if?"

Be careful what you wish for, though! In "Rumpelstiltskin," soon after the miller's daughter meets the elfin man able to turn straw into gold, she discovers, as every fairy-tale hero and heroine eventually does, that magic always comes at a price. What precious possession will she trade for his help? What is it worth to her? What would *we* trade? Fairy tales challenge us to decide what we hold dear. They value values and offer parents and children chance after chance to talk about happiness, friendship, envy, honesty, cooperation, greed, loyalty, love—

the building blocks of all that it means to be human.

If the stories gathered in *Mary Engelbreit's Fairy Tales* have a common thread, it is the very fine and basic notion that love matters: love stumbled upon when least expected ("Cinderella," "Beauty and the Beast"), love longed for ("Rapunzel"), lost ("The Little Mermaid"), and found ("Snow White"). A second common thread of this colorful treasury has to do with . . . threads: the grandly elaborate enterprise that the artist, as always, has made of dressing her characters in fanciful polka dot, paisley, and floral patterned costumes. The intricately detailed drawings are fun to savor while enjoying the theatrical flair Mary Engelbreit brings to the tales. The curtain goes up and we're suddenly immersed in a minidrama pitting an envious stepmother or greedy king against the good young person who must navigate the thickets of some unimaginably devious plan. The curtain goes down and we're back home safe and sound again—a tad the wiser perhaps, entertained for sure, and left with a timeless question to carry us off to sleep: "What if?"

—Leonard S. Marcus

Author, critic, and children's literature historian

Welcome!

Once upon a time, I fell in love with the delightful world of fairy tales. Stories of princesses and their princes, danger, magic, and happily ever afters have stayed with me my entire life. I hope you'll be enchanted, too!

Mary EngelBreit

CINDERELLA

Once there was a girl named Ella who was good and kind and beautiful—but her stepmother was vain and selfish, and her two stepsisters were just as bad. They made Ella do all the hard work. Since she was often covered in dirt and cinders, they called her Cinderella.

One night the Prince was
having a grand ball, but Cinderella's
stepmother would not let her go.
Alone and lonely, Cinderella began
to cry. Her tears were falling freely
when her fairy godmother appeared.
Tapping things with her magic wand, the
fairy godmother changed a pumpkin into a
splendid coach. Six mice turned into horses,
and a rat became the coachman.

Then the fairy godmother touched
Cinderella with her wand. Instantly, instead
of rags Cinderella wore a pink gown and silver
slippers. Smiling, the fairy godmother said,
"Do not stay late at the ball, my dear, for at
the stroke of midnight, the magic will
end, and all will be as it was before."

When Cinderella arrived at the ball, everyone stopped to stare. Her stepsisters, who did not recognize her, were jealous. The Prince thought Cinderella was the most beautiful woman he had ever seen, and he asked her to dance all through the night. She was having so much fun that she forgot to think about the time.

Bong! Bong! Bong! The clock began to strike midnight. Suddenly, Cinderella ran out the door and down the steps. One of her silver slippers fell off, but she kept running. As the clock struck twelve, her beautiful gown turned to rags, and her coach disappeared! All she had left was one silver slipper.

The Prince was very sad. When he found a
silver slipper on the palace steps, he and his
men traveled throughout the kingdom, trying
the slipper on every lady's foot.

At last the slipper was brought to Cinderella's ugly stepsisters. They pinched their heels
and curled their toes, but the slipper didn't fit.
Then Cinderella said softly, "May I try?"

The Prince ran in to find that
the slipper fit her perfectly.

When he took one look into Cinderella's good, kind face, he knew she was his Princess. It was a grand wedding. Cinderella and her Prince danced well past midnight, and they enjoyed each other's company ever after.

BEAUTY and the BEAST

One day a man set out from home to seek his fortune. He promised his three daughters to bring back as many presents as he could and asked them what they would like. "Diamonds!" said one. "Dresses!" said another. But the youngest, Beauty, asked only for a rose.

The man had not traveled very far when he came to a castle with beautiful gardens. Remembering his daughter's wish, he stopped and picked a single rose.

As he did, a frightful beast rushed into the garden. "Thief!" The beast roared. "How dare you steal my roses?"

"I'm sorry!" the man said. "I only wanted a rose for my daughter Beauty."

"A daughter?" said the Beast. He thought for a moment. "If your daughter willingly comes to live in my castle, I will spare your life. But if she will not, you will die."

The man was so frightened that he went straight home. When she heard what had happened, Beauty said, "Father, we must not let the Beast harm you. I will go." And though her father tried to stop her, Beauty went to the Beast's castle.

Beauty was frightened at first, but she was well cared for at the castle. She had only to wish for something—a meal, a dress, a jewel—and it appeared. In the evenings, the Beast came to have dinner with Beauty. He was frightful to look at, but she enjoyed his company and saw the goodness in his heart.

Every night before leaving her, the Beast would ask, "Beauty, will you marry me?"

She always answered, "No, Beast. I cannot marry you, for I do not love you."

One day, after many months had gone by, the Beast said, "If you cannot marry me, promise you will never leave. For I would die if you ever left me."

Beauty said, "I promise I will stay with you forever if only I can see my family for one more week."

Believing her, the Beast gave her a magic ring and said, "Put this on your finger. You will be home in an instant. At the end of seven days, place it back on your finger and it will bring you here. If you stay longer, dear Beauty, I will die."

Promising to return, Beauty put the ring on her finger.

The next moment she was surrounded by her family. So happy was she to be home that seven, then eight, then nine days passed before Beauty realized it.

On the tenth night, she had a terrible dream. In it, the Beast lay dying by a river. She woke, saying, "My poor Beast!" And placing the ring on her finger, she was instantly back at the Beast's castle.

Beauty raced to the stream, where she found the Beast lying barely alive.

She cradled his head and whispered, "Oh, Beast. You cannot die, because I cannot live without you. I love you."

As she spoke the words, the light of the sun broke through the clouds and the Beast awoke. Then, right before her eyes, the Beast changed into a handsome young Prince.

"A wicked fairy cast a spell on me," explained the Prince. "I had to remain an ugly beast until I could find someone to love me for my goodness alone. Oh, Beauty, will you marry me?"

"I will," Beauty said. "I loved you even as you were, and I will love you forevermore."

And they lived happily ever after.

ALADDIN

nce there was a poor young man named Aladdin who was hopelessly in love with a Sultan's daughter. Whenever Princess Aria passed by, his heart stopped. Aladdin knew that a poor boy could never win a Sultan's daughter, but he swore that he would never love another.

Next to the
Princess, what
Aladdin loved most
was exploring. One day
he discovered a hidden cave,
and inside he found an old oil lamp.
This was no ordinary lamp—it had been
hidden in the cave by a wicked and
powerful magician.

It was a dusty thing, and Aladdin
began to polish it with his sleeve. All
of a sudden . . . WHOOSH! A burst of
light filled the cave, and out of the
lamp a genie appeared.

"Master of the lamp," the genie
boomed. "What is your wish?"

Aladdin was astonished!
And he knew just what to
ask for. He said, "I wish
for a gift fine enough
for Princess Aria."

No sooner had he said the words than Aladdin found himself surrounded by riches. "Your wish is my command," said the genie. "What else do you desire?"

Aladdin wished for fine clothes and a good steed.

Soon dressed in princely clothes and riding a fine stallion, he was off to the Sultan's palace.

The Sultan and his daughter were charmed by Aladdin's friendly smile. After an enchanting afternoon, Princess Aria agreed to marry him.

Aladdin commanded the genie to build them a grand palace, and in an instant it was done. Happy beyond measure, Aladdin still told no one, not even his dear Aria, about the magic lamp.

One day, when Aladdin was away, the Princess found the dusty lamp high on a shelf. Hours later a peddler came walking through the streets crying, "New lamps for old! New lamps for old!"

"Will you take even this old tarnished one?" the Princess asked.

"Certainly!" came the reply. For this man was not a peddler; he was the wicked magician who had hidden the lamp in the cave. And he was determined to get it back.

As soon as he held the lamp, he rubbed it, and the genie appeared. "Carry this palace and all of us in it far into the desert," the magician commanded. In an instant, only bare ground remained where the palace had stood.

When Aladdin returned home, he realized at once what must have happened. Without wasting a minute, he set out to find and rescue Princess Aria.

After wandering the desert for weeks, Aladdin discovered the palace. He snuck inside and surprised his bride. Aria was overcome with joy to see him.

"We must get the lamp," said Aladdin. The Princess said, "It's always by his side."

So that night, as the magician slept, Aladdin crept into his room. He took the lamp and made a wish.

When the magician awoke, he was asleep in the sand!

Back in the city, Aladdin and the Princess thanked the genie for all his help. The Sultan was so happy that he gave Aladdin half his kingdom. From then on, Aladdin used the lamp only to do good for his people, and he shared his great riches with the poor.

SNOW WHITE and the SEVEN DWARFS

nce there was a lovely princess called

Snow White. Her stepmother, the queen, was

beautiful but very vain. The Queen loved to look

into her magic mirror and say:

Mirror, mirror on the wall,

Who is fairest of us all?

And the mirror always said:
Queen, you are fairest of us all.
But Snow White grew more beautiful as she grew older, and one day the mirror said:

Queen, thou art fairest that I see,
But Snow White is more fair than thee.

Furious, the Queen called to her guard and ordered him to kill Snow White.

The guard could not bear to hurt the innocent girl and simply took her deep into the woods, where he left her all alone. But he told the Queen that Snow White was dead.

Poor Snow White wandered through the frightening woods for a long while.

At last she came to a little cottage.

She knocked timidly at the door—and was surprised when it was opened by the tiniest person she had ever seen!

The cottage was owned by seven friendly dwarfs. When they learned what the wicked Queen had done to Snow White, they offered to let her live with them.

Snow White agreed, and they settled into a happy routine. Each morning the dwarfs would go off to work, and each evening they would return to warm supper and a house as neat as a pin.

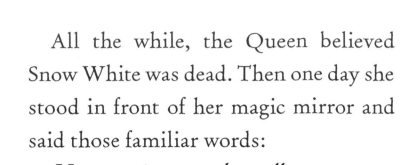

All the while, the Queen believed Snow White was dead. Then one day she stood in front of her magic mirror and said those familiar words:

Mirror, mirror on the wall,
Who is fairest of us all?
And the mirror answered:
Queen, thou art fairest that I see,
But Snow White living in the glen
With the seven little men
Is a thousand times more fair than thee.

Imagine how shocked and angry the Queen was!
With magic spells she created a poisonous apple.

Then she disguised herself as an old peddler and set off for the seven dwarfs' cottage. Once there, she called out, "Apples for sale. Delicious apples."

Snow White told the old woman she had no money.

"For one so pretty as you, the apple is free," the old woman said.

Snow White could not resist. She took the apple and bit into it. As soon as she did, she fell down, still and cold.

The Queen laughed with glee and disappeared into the woods.

When the seven dwarfs came home, they were heartbroken to find their dear Snow White lying there.

She looked too beautiful to bury, so they placed
her in a glass coffin atop a high hill. Each dwarf took
a turn keeping watch.

Snow White lay there for a long, long time. But
her appearance never changed. She seemed only to be
sleeping.

One day, a king's son rode by and was charmed by Snow White's beauty. He begged the dwarfs to move the coffin so he could see her better. As they picked it up, the bit of apple fell out of her mouth and she awoke.

Seeing Snow White's lovely face made the Prince joyful. They walked and talked and soon fell in love.

The seven dwarfs were the guests of honor at the grand celebration of their marriage. A great feast was held, and Snow White danced with everyone. Before the night ended, she and the Prince made the dwarfs promise to visit them often at the castle.

And so they all lived happily ever after.

the FROG PRINCE

Once you could always find the Princess

alone, playing with her golden ball by the pond on

the castle grounds. One day she missed her catch,

and the ball landed in the pond and sank.

The Princess didn't want to wade in to get the ball.

She didn't want to get wet! So she began to cry.

A small green frog asked, "What will you give me if I get the ball for you?"

"You can have anything you want," she said.

"What I want is simply to be your friend. I want to sit with you at supper and eat from your plate. I want to listen as you read aloud from a book and to sleep on your pillow after you kiss me good night."

Well, the Princess was sure her father the King would not welcome a warty old frog to dinner, but she promised anyway. As soon as the Frog brought her the golden ball, the Princess skipped away to the palace, ignoring the Frog's ribbet-y cries to wait for him.

By dinnertime, the Frog had hopped all the way to the castle, where he called out for the Princess.

"What would a frog want with you?" the King asked his daughter.

And so the Princess told him she'd promised the Frog she'd be his friend if only he would return the golden ball to her.

"A promise made must be kept," said the King.

So the Frog joined the royal family for dinner. He ate from the young princess's plate and drank from her cup. After dinner, the Princess read to him from her storybook. Much to the Princess's surprise, the Frog was good company, and they passed a pleasant evening together.

At bedtime the Princess carried the Frog up the stairs and set him on her pillow. But she had no wish to share her pillow with a frog, even a nice frog. So she said, "You may sleep on my pillow. I will gladly sleep here on the floor." She kissed him on his knobby head and said, "Good night, my dear Froggy."

In that instant, the Frog turned into a handsome Prince. The Princess could not believe her eyes, but the Prince explained that a witch had put a spell on him, and the Princess was the first to break it with a kiss.

Now they could play and talk for hours, and they grew to be very fond of each other. Best of all, the Princess had someone to play catch with—and they never tired of tossing each other the golden ball that had brought them together.

the LITTLE MERMAID

Out at sea, there lived a good mer-king with his six daughters in a palace made of coral and shells. Happy in their underwater kingdom, the mermaid princesses played among the flowers on the sea floor. Only the youngest wondered what it would be like to walk on land.

One day, after a shipwreck, the Little Mermaid rescued the only survivor, a handsome prince. The Little Mermaid pulled the Prince to the shore—but there she had to leave him. She could not go on land herself. Instead she kept watch from the waves a short distance away.

The next morning, a lovely girl came across the Prince asleep on the beach. When he awoke, he thought that this girl had saved him. He remembered nothing of the Little Mermaid.

But the Little Mermaid could not forget the Prince.

She returned to the edge of the shore every day, hoping to see him. She wanted to be with him, but she knew that a prince would never love a princess with a fish's tail.

So the Little Mermaid went to visit the Old Witch of the Sea.

"My help comes with a high price," said the Witch, giving the Little Mermaid a small bottle. "If you drink this potion, you will become human, but you will lose your voice. And if the Prince does not marry you, you will turn to sea foam and disappear forever." Unafraid, the Little Mermaid drank the potion and fainted dead away.

When she awoke in human form, she saw the Prince but could not speak. Seeing that she needed help, the Prince took her to his castle. From that day on, the Little Mermaid was happy just to be near him.

But the Prince decided to marry the girl he believed had rescued him from the sea.

The Little Mermaid could not
speak to tell him the truth. When she saw how
happy he was, she did not want to.

On the night of the wedding, the Little
Mermaid walked along the shore, staring out
to sea. Through her tears, she saw her sisters rise
up through the waves. "We have come from the
Old Witch of the Sea," one said. "If you kill the
Prince before sunrise, you may return to the
world under the waves."

Then they handed her a magic dagger.

Of course, the Little Mermaid could not harm the Prince. She threw away the dagger and jumped into the sea. She expected to turn into foam, but instead, she felt herself rising into the air, surrounded by friendly spirits. "You have done many kind things for others," the spirits said. "Come stay with us, and be happy forever."

At once, the Little Mermaid was happy. She had dreamed of walking, but now she could fly.

the PRINCESS and the PEA

Once upon a time, there was a prince who wanted more than anything to fall in love and get married. But though he met one princess after another, there was always something not quite right.

"They just aren't real princesses," he said. "They aren't real princesses at all!"

"What is a real princess?" asked his father, the King.

"Her hair will shine, her nose will be regal, but the princess part will be in her eyes. They'll sparkle," said the Prince.

"And fine! A princess will be fine," added his mother, who had once been a princess herself, of course.

Now, one evening a wild
storm broke over the kingdom.
Suddenly there came a knock at the palace
door. Outside stood a girl, soaking wet
from head to toe.

"Who are you?" asked the King.

"I am Princess Adriana and I got
separated from my companions in the
storm," she said.

The Prince came running. It was hard to see if she was a real princess. Her nose looked regal, but water dripped from the tip of it. And her eyes—the Prince could hardly see them behind the mop of wet hair.

Now the Queen knew that a true princess would be very, very delicate, and she thought of a way to test the girl's claim. She gathered all the mattresses and quilts from all the beds in the palace and stacked them up.

Then she secretly tucked a tiny pea under the bottom mattress and bid the girl good night.

When the girl came downstairs in the morning, she was a lovely sight to see. Her hair flowed long and wavy, washed clean from the rain. Her nose was just as regal as could be. And when she looked up—

"Your eyes! They're so sparkly!" said the Prince.

"But you are yawning!" said the Queen. "Didn't you sleep well, my dear?"

"You were wonderful to take me in, and I don't like to complain," said the girl, "but I did not sleep a wink! There was a lump in the bed, and I'm afraid it kept me awake all night."

"Aha!" cried the Queen. "You are a real princess! Only a real princess could be fine enough to feel a pea through twenty mattresses!"

The Prince quickly fell in love with the Princess. In time they got married and the Prince started making the bed every day, careful to smooth out any lumps or wrinkles so that his dear Princess would enjoy a good night's sleep.

RAPUNZEL

One day, a witch stole a little baby from her parents. She named the girl Rapunzel and locked her in a tall tower deep in the woods. The tower had no door, no stairs, and only a small window at the top. Rapunzel lived alone there for many years. Her golden hair grew so long it reached the ground.

When the Witch wanted to visit, she would stand below the window and shout, "Rapunzel, Rapunzel! Let down your hair!"

Rapunzel would lower her long golden braid, and the Witch would use it as a rope to climb the tower wall.

One day, a king's son rode nearby when Rapunzel was singing to her only companions, the birds. Hearing Rapunzel's beautiful voice, he drew closer to the tower. He was just in time to see the Witch arrive and hear her shout, "Rapunzel, Rapunzel! Let down your hair!"

Hiding behind a tree, the Prince saw the golden braid cascade down from the window for the Witch to climb.

As soon as the Witch had gone, the Prince hurried to the foot of the tower and called, "Rapunzel, Rapunzel! Let down your hair!"

Rapunzel was surprised and delighted to see a young prince. She welcomed him happily.

The Prince returned every evening to visit, and as they talked and sang together, they fell in love. They planned to marry as soon as Rapunzel could escape from the tower.

But one day, when Rapunzel was
lost in dreams, she forgot herself and
foolishly asked the Witch, "Why do
you climb so much slower than my
Prince?"

Realizing she'd been tricked,
the Witch grew furious.

She took out a big pair of scissors
and lopped off Rapunzel's long
braid with one mighty snip.
  Then she took Rapunzel to
a faraway wilderness and left
her there, all alone.

That evening, the Witch returned to the tower. When the Prince called, "Rapunzel, Rapunzel! Let down your hair!" the braid came tumbling down as usual. But when the Prince reached the window, there was the Witch!

"Your sweet songbird has left the nest," she screeched. "You'll never see her again!" She pushed the Prince out of the tower, and he fell into a patch of briars that scratched out his eyes.

Blind and lonely, the Prince wandered far and wide, always searching for Rapunzel. He'd nearly given up hope when one day he heard a soft, sad song that he recognized from long ago.

Running toward the sound, he cried out, "Rapunzel!" Rapunzel fell against him, crying tears of happiness. And what happened then was truly magical. When her tears fell into his eyes, he found he could see again! What he saw was his one true love.

Soon Rapunzel and her Prince
were married. Her hair once
again grew long, and her
joyous song filled their
castle like sunshine.

THUMBELINA

Once upon a time, a tiny maiden named Thumbelina lived in a garden. She made her home under a flower. Her bed was a walnut shell, and she had a rose leaf for a blanket. Thumbelina loved living in the garden. All of the bumblebees and dragonflies were her friends.

One night, a toad crept through the garden, saw Thumbelina sleeping, and thought, What a pretty little wife she will make for my son! Picking up the bed with Thumbelina in it, the toad hopped away.

When Thumbelina awoke, she found herself on a lily pad far out in a stream. Two large toads were staring at her. The older one told Thumbelina, "Meet my son. He will be your husband."

"Croak, croak!" her son said, tipping his hat.

Thumbelina couldn't bear to think of marrying the toad. As the mother and son swam away, she began to cry. Luckily fish had been listening nearby, and they felt sorry for Thumbelina. They sent her lily pad floating downstream.

Thumbelina sailed past many towns, finally reaching a beautiful country.

There she wove a bed from blades of grass, drank the dew from the leaves, and ate the honey from the flowers. When the first snow came, Thumbelina took shelter with a field mouse.

One day, the mouse took Thumbelina to call on a very rich neighbor, the mole. As they walked through a tunnel to his grand underground home, they came across a dead swallow. Thumbelina was very sad, but the mole just said, "How glad I am not to be a bird." He ordered his workers to cover up the hole in the tunnel roof through which the swallow had fallen.

That night Thumbelina could not sleep. Taking a blanket, she crept out of bed to the tunnel. "Farewell, dear one," she whispered. Spreading the warm blanket over the swallow's cold body, she laid her head on the bird's breast. But what do you think she heard then? The thump of a heartbeat! The bird was not really dead, only frozen, and the blanket had warmed him back to life.

All that winter and on into spring, Thumbelina secretly visited the swallow, bringing him food and drink. Then one day she rushed to him crying, "The mole wants to marry me!"

Knowing that Thumbelina didn't want to marry the mole any more than she had wanted to marry the toad, the swallow said, "Fly away with me."

Thumbelina quickly agreed. She climbed on his back, and away they flew!

After many days, the bird set Thumbelina down gently in a field of flowers. As tiny people who lived among the blossoms rushed up and welcomed her, Thumbelina felt warm and happy. Finally she had come home.

SNOW WHITE and ROSE RED

Once a poor widow lived with her two daughters in a little cottage close by the big woods. Beautiful red and white rosebushes bloomed all around their cozy home. The woman loved the roses so much that she had named her daughters for them, Snow White and Rose Red.

One snowy evening, there was a heavy knock at the cottage door. When the widow opened it, she saw an enormous bear! He looked frightening, but he spoke in a gentle voice and said, "May I come in out of the storm?"

It was too cold to make the poor bear sleep outside, so Snow White and Rose Red brushed the snow off him and invited him to come in.

From that day on, all through the winter, the bear was like one of the family. He slept near the hearth every night.

But when spring came,
he thanked them and said, "I must
find a wicked dwarf who stole my treasure
and cast a spell on me." And off he went with
a wave and a smile.

A few days later, Snow White and Rose Red came
across a dwarf whose long beard was snagged on
the bark of a fallen tree.

"Why don't you help me instead of
standing there like ninnies!" the
little man shouted.

Rose Red tugged with all her might but
could not pull the beard out.

"Worthless!" shouted the dwarf.
"You're no more helpful than
a toadstool!"

"Don't be impatient," said Snow White
kindly. "I will free you." And with that,
she took a pair of scissors out of her bag
and snipped off the end of his beard.

As soon as he was free, the dwarf ran at them, shaking
his fist. "Go away!" he shouted. "You've no business
here!" Then he grabbed a bag of gold he had
hidden nearby and hurried away, grumbling,
"Beastly children. You've ruined my beard!"

Just then, a bear came roaring out of the forest.
He knocked the dwarf to the ground with one
swipe of his mighty paw.

The sisters started to run away, but
then a familiar voice called, "Snow White!
Rose Red! Wait!" This was the very bear they
had befriended the winter before!

As it walked toward them, its fur fell away, revealing a handsome young man. "I am the King's son," the young man said. "I was under a spell cast by that wicked dwarf, forced to roam the woods as a bear until I could find him again."

The sisters took the Prince home to see their mother. They were all very happy to be together again and celebrated with a picnic near the rosebushes.

RUMPELSTILTSKIN

nce a miller bragged about his lovely

daughter to the King. He claimed that she could do

anything! "She can even spin straw into gold!" The

miller didn't mean to lie; it just popped out.

"Bring her to my castle," said the King hastily. "My

advisers demand more gold."

So the Miller brought his daughter to the castle. When the King saw her, he fell in love, but his advisers locked the poor girl in a room full of straw, saying, "Spin this straw into gold by morning. If you cannot, then your father will be put to death for lying to the King."

The poor girl knew she couldn't spin that straw into gold. When she began to cry, a tiny little man appeared. He promised to spin the gold if she would give him something in return.

"My necklace?" the girl offered.

The little man agreed, and in no time he spun all the straw into gold.

The King was amazed and thanked the girl, but his advisers locked her into an even bigger room full of straw and demanded more gold.

Once more the tiny little man appeared. Again he promised to spin the gold in return for something.

"My ring?" the girl offered.

The little man agreed, and again he spun every bit of straw into gold.

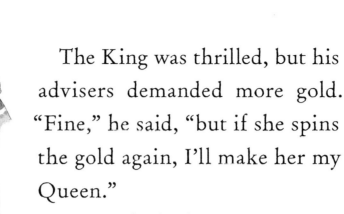

The King was thrilled, but his advisers demanded more gold. "Fine," he said, "but if she spins the gold again, I'll make her my Queen."

Again the little man appeared, but now the girl had nothing left to give him.

"I will spin the gold," said the little man, "if you promise to give me your firstborn child." The girl believed she would never have a child because she thought the advisers would never let her marry.

"Very well," she said. "I agree."

When the King's advisers saw all the gold, they were delighted. And when the King embraced the Miller's daughter, he swore that he would love her always. They were married, and in time the new Queen gave birth to a baby boy, who was the joy of her life. But on the boy's first birthday, the tiny little man appeared once more.

The Queen begged and pleaded to keep her child. The little man finally agreed to release her from her promise only if she could guess his name in three days' time. On the first day, the Queen tried name after name, but to each the little man shook his head. On the second day, the Queen sent her servants out to gather every name in the kingdom. Still, she couldn't guess.

On the third day, she had almost given up hope when one of her handmaids came running into the room. She had been walking in the woods when she overheard the little man singing:

What a most delightful game,
Oh, Rumpelstiltskin is my name!

That evening, the little man came to claim his prize. The Queen asked, "Is your name Peter?"

"No," he replied.

"John?"

"No."

"Ralph?"

"No!"

"Albert?"

"No!!"

Now the Queen smiled.
"Is it . . . Rumpelstiltskin?"

At that, Rumpelstiltskin stamped his little feet and flew into a rage.

He ran away as fast as his legs could carry him, and he was never seen again.

SLEEPING BEAUTY

On the occasion of their first baby's birth, a king and queen invited six good fairies to a party. They forgot to invite the seventh fairy!

At the party, the fairies began to give gifts to the Princess. The first wished her wisdom. The second, a kind heart. The third, great beauty.

And so it went up through the fifth fairy, with each
one offering a gift to assure the Princess a happy life.

Suddenly the door to the castle flew open. It was
the seventh fairy, and she was furious.

"Now I will give my gift to the Princess," she said.
"When she is fifteen years old, she will prick her finger
on a spinning wheel and fall down dead."

Then the angry fairy stormed out of the room.

The King and Queen were terribly upset. But then the sixth fairy, who was the youngest of all, stepped forward.

"I have not yet given my gift," she said. "I cannot change the wicked curse, but I can soften it. The Princess will not die but instead will fall into a deep sleep. She will awaken only when her true love kisses her."

The King was grateful to the young fairy but still worried. Trying to avoid the curse, he decreed that every spinning wheel in the kingdom be burned in a great fire.

Many years passed, and just as the good fairies wished, the Princess grew to be kind and smart and beautiful. The wicked curse was all but forgotten.

On the day she turned fifteen, the Princess decided to explore the castle. Coming to a tower she'd never seen before, she climbed its winding staircase and opened the door at the top. Inside was a woman sitting at a spinning wheel. The Princess didn't know it, but the woman was the wicked fairy in disguise.

"What are you doing?" asked the Princess. She had never seen a spinning wheel, since they had all been burned.

"I'm spinning flax into thread," said the woman, smiling. "Would you like to try?"

The Princess sat down at the spinning wheel, but no sooner had she touched it than she pricked her finger on the sharp spindle. Instantly, she fell into a deep sleep.

In fact, the angry fairy's spell was so strong that dogs stopped barking, flies stopped buzzing, and curtains stopped flapping in the breeze. The King and Queen and every creature in the castle fell asleep. A tangled hedge of thorns grew around the castle walls, so thick that no one could enter.

And then one day, a hundred years later, a prince came riding by. Although many men had tried and failed to fight their way through the hedge, this prince was special. He was Beauty's true love. As he approached the hedge, its branches parted and he rode straight to the castle.

Everywhere he looked, he saw people and animals
fast asleep.

He tiptoed among them until, finally, he found the
sleeping Princess in the tower.

He thought she was so beautiful that he leaned over and kissed her cheek. And just like that, the spell was broken.

Opening her eyes, the Princess said, "I dreamed you would come." Then she took his hand, and they came down from the tower to find the whole kingdom waking up.

The King and the Queen were so overjoyed that they planned a great feast to at last celebrate the Princess's sixteenth birthday. And this time, they made sure to invite every single fairy in the wood.

A NOTE FROM MARY

Imagining these pictures, I was filled with nostalgia; it was the fulfillment of a dream to draw the princesses and scenes that were such a part of my childhood. I love fairy tales and wanted to create a treasury that would celebrate those early memories.

Everyone has a favorite—a special story they remember best. My sister Alexa loved "Rumpelstiltskin" and would ask my mother to read it every single night. My mother's own favorite was "Snow White and Rose Red." She was very close to her own sister, and perhaps that's why she loved that story so. I couldn't get enough of "Snow White and the Seven Dwarfs" because they lived in that secret woodland that I drew over and over when I was little. My earliest drawings are actually scenes from my favorite stories. I would spend hours trying to perfect an elf or a giant. I loved "Thumbelina" and creating that miniaturized world.

I wanted to share these timeless stories with children today, but as I read and considered which to include, I realized for the first time how many of the stories ended with the message that marrying a prince is the solution to all of life's problems. If only that were true! Knowing how independent and free-spirited my daughter Mikayla and her friends are—and wanting to nurture that—I felt it was important to bring out the spirit of dashing

adventure in the richly imaginative world that I'd enjoyed as a child. So I decided to edit some of these endings a bit, letting children know it is okay for the princess and her frog to remain friends or that a prince can help with the household chores.

After choosing the twelve tales, I had fun dreaming up the costumes, especially the ball gowns. I based the clothes on styles, decorative patterns, and fabrics from different periods that I like, especially Elizabethan and medieval times.

Then I began the drawings. I'd sketch the whole story at once to make sure that I was keeping the characters and settings consistent and staying in the mood. Maintaining consistency within each story became tricky, for me at least, because the dresses became so elaborate! Once I was satisfied with my sketches, I inked the drawings. Then I began to color. Once I was in that part of the process, I would color the stories for days at a time.

Mikayla, like most little girls, identifies with the pretty young princesses and likes to imagine she could be one of them. It was fun to hear her thoughts about many of the characters and situations as I worked on the scenes, and that leads me to hope that as you read with your loved ones, you'll also find much in these pictures to talk about and share.